I0819829

This is a work of fiction and meant for entertainment. Any similarity to actual persons, places, or events is coincidence and not intentional.

Hardcover ISBN 978-0-578-92677-3

Written by Puente Verdad
Illustrations by Jakob Page
Cover Art by Jakob Page
Printed by IngramSpark 2021

Match Tea Books

AND TO THINK I SAW IT ON MLK STREET

By Puente Verdad

Illustrations by
Jacob Page

I wake up each morning and break my fast.
It's time for school, I make a mad dash.
"Not so fast," my dad might say,
"It's lovely outside, take the long way!"
Walk slow and enjoy the time on your feet,
and take in the sights on MLK Street"

“But dad don’t you know, it’s scary outside?
There’s dangerous people, please give me a ride!”
My father would say, “turn off the news and you might be surprised, the things that are scary are inside your mind.
So walk down the street, don’t look at your phone,
If you see something bad, just run on back home.”

I head on my way, shoes tight on my feet,
Determined to brave MLK Street.
My dad will feel sorry when I tell him tonight,
The sights that I see will give him a fright...

On MLK the first thing that I see...
Well this isn't scary, it's a regular scene.
Happy people moving in flocks,
I need to scare dad out of his socks!
People handshaking and sharing a hug,
No gloves and no masks, they could spread the bug!
Well this just won't do!
They could catch the flu!

I should go home, I should be inside.
Any sane person would stay home and hide.
But that won't convince dad I had to retreat
That's just the first block on MLK Street...

Next on my way, you won't believe what I found!
It's easy to see I followed the sound.
"This isn't scary," I think in my head.
I heard a loud bang, I thought I'd be dead!
Someone's car tire went pop,
The person to help him first was a cop.

I need something scary, more than a car
I don't need to stretch the story too far.
The cop shot at him, it's easy to see
The color of his skin is different from me.
This will convince dad it's scary outside,
Oh how he'll wish he gave me a ride!

But that's not all I happened to meet,
the day I walked down MLK Street...

On the next corner I saw a man,
With a stack of flyers in his hand.
He had a red hat and seemed perfectly nice
But I know that it was just a disguise.
"Vote for my guy," he said with a smile
But what I heard was nasty and vile.

I know the hat that was on his head,
Is just the same as an armband in red.
He yelled and he screamed of something he knew,
How banks and TV are controlled by a few.
I ran and I ran away from that place!
To make it to school I had to keep pace.
The next thing I know my school is in sight.
But something that blocked me gave me a fright...

A steeple stretched high, its people outside
Shouting, “We’re going to heaven, come along for the ride!”
“Free food at noon, please come one and all!”
However I know that’s not why they call.
They seem nice at first, so you won’t see
That these people hate people like me.

They say babies need rights, please do not plan it.
But I know that tykes are bad for the planet.
They say they accept you for you,
But I know that those words just are not true.
They'll take all your money and then they'll take
more, What else would they invite you in for?

So I ran and I ran, I finally made it.
I couldn't believe the things I evaded.

In my classroom I'm happy to find
Both students and teachers who share my same mind.

They know the truth, they see as I see,
So I told them my story and they applaud me.

So I called my dad at the end of the day,
I couldn't wait for what I wanted to say.
"How was your walk? Who did you
meet?"

I froze...

"I saw nothing scary on MLK Street."

www.ingramcontent.com/pod-product-compliance
Lightning Source LLC
Chambersburg PA
CBHW070619310726
48982CB00001B/124
9780578926773